Elephant in a Well

Elephant in a Well

Written and illustrated by

Marie Hall Ets

THE VIKING PRESS   NEW YORK

FOR MARJORIE HALL HUGHES—

WHO KNOWS MORE ABOUT

CHILDREN'S BOOKS THAN I DO

Copyright © 1972 by Marie Hall Ets

All rights reserved
Viking Seafarer edition issued in 1973 by The Viking Press, Inc.
625 Madison Avenue, New York, N.Y. 10022
Distributed in Canada by
The Macmillan Company of Canada Limited
Printed in U.S.A.

Pic Bk

Library of Congress catalog card number: 74–183935
SBN 670–05084–9.

2   3   4   5   77   76   75   74

Once when Young Elephant was wandering about
with a clothesline wound around her trunk

she fell into a well and

SHE COULDN'T GET OUT.

Horse came along and wanted to help.

Horse pulled on the rope with all his might.
But Horse alone couldn't pull Young Elephant out of the well.

Then Cow came along and wanted to help.

So Horse and Cow both pulled and pulled.
But Horse and Cow together couldn't pull Young Elephant out of the well.

Then Goat came along and wanted to help.
So Horse and Cow and Goat all pulled.

But Horse and Cow and Goat together
couldn't pull Young Elephant out of the well.

Then Pig came along and wanted to help.

So Horse and Cow and Goat and Pig all pulled.

But Horse and Cow and Goat and Pig together

couldn't pull Young Elephant out of the well.

Then Lamb came along and wanted to help.
So Horse and Cow and Goat and Pig and Lamb all pulled.

But Horse and Cow and Goat and Pig and Lamb together
couldn't pull Young Elephant out of the well.

Then Dog came along and wanted to help.

So Horse and Cow and Goat and Pig and Lamb and Dog all pulled.

But Horse and Cow and Goat and Pig and Lamb and Dog together

couldn't pull Young Elephant out of the well.

Then Mouse came out and wanted to help.

And Horse and Cow and Goat and Pig and Lamb and Dog all laughed.

But Horse and Cow and Goat and Pig and Lamb and Dog

AND Mouse did pull Young Elephant out of the well.

And she never fell in again.